What Happened with June

# What Happened with June

초판 1쇄 발행일 | 2020년 4월 1일

지은이  |  김학진
펴낸이  |  김동명
펴낸곳  |  도서출판 창조와 지식
디자인  |  주식회사 북모아
인쇄처  |  주식회사 북모아

출판등록번호  |  제2018-000027호
주소  |  서울특별시 강북구 덕릉로 144
전화  |  1644-1814
팩스  |  02-2275-8577

ISBN 979-11-6003-217-8   03840

지식의 가치를 창조하는 도서출판 창조와 지식
www.mybookmake.com

What
Happened
with
June

HakJin Kim

## Characters

- June Kee
- John Kee
- Mrs. Sara Kee, née Miller
- Lan Kee (June's paternal grandmother)

- Don Johnson (June's future boyfriend)
- Graciela (Don's mother)
- Alice (Don's cousin)
- Maria (Graciela's mother)

- Jennifer Chang (June's best friend)

- Brent (Don's roommate)

On a sunny day in late August, a brand new car pulls to a stop in a well groomed driveway. A teenage girl opens the driver's door and smiles at a woman sitting in the passenger seat. Soon the woman gets out and stands next to the girl.

"June, you drove along nice and easy. How do you feel about your first car?" Maria, the woman, asks.

"It's perfect for me. I love Malibu. It looks nicer here," June, the teenage girl, says with excitement.

"It's a lovely car. I like it too. Now what? Are you gonna drive to somewhere without me?" Maria asks, smiling.

"Not now. I'm tired a bit. I think I was nervous. Maria, are you leaving now?" June asks.

"Yes, I have errands to run for Sara. Oh, I texted her we

arrived at home," Maria says.

"Thanks. See you tomorrow," June says.

As soon as Maria goes to her car, June gets in her Malibu to pull it into the garage. After closing the garage door, June goes up the stairs to her room. She flings herself on the bed and begins to imagine that she drives alone on the freeway, feeling more excited then more.

Less than a minute June opens her eyes and looks at an abstract shaped mobile hanging from the ceiling. While watching its gentle swaying, she feels at peace. June knows that she has been loved all the time as the only daughter of Sara and John Kee. June has never been upset and grew up to be a nice girl who tries to conform to her parents' demand. As time goes on, June becomes mature in gratitude for her family's support and Maria.

Speaking of Maria, she has been with Kee's family since June turned nine years old. She has been like June's aunt by doing things for June such as giving a ride and spending time together. Maria has been reliable and hard-working. June believes in Maria over almost everything. Now Maria is working for Sara, who began her e-commerce fashion startup several years ago, by commuting to and from work by her car and attends to family matters for June when necessary.

While June is still in the mood, she also thinks of her grandmother who was always on June's side. Since she moved to Seoul a couple of years ago due to the loss of her husband, June only texts her grandmother whenever something has come up.

A little while later June jumps to her feet as if there is something to do. She takes out her cell phone from her backpack and sits on the built-in couch by the window the sun shines in.

As she looks down at the neatly planted garden, a boy comes into view. He is passing her house on the sidewalk by riding his tricycle next to an elderly woman who looks like his grandmother. June watches them until they disappear from view.

A few minutes have passed, and the boy who passed by comes to her mind. And then memories of her childhood flashes through her mind. June remembers the boy who sat next to her in class on the first day of school. As a first grader everybody was a stranger to June, but the boy looked familiar giving her a feeling of comfort. Due to his small eyes she thought he was born to a Korean and American family like she was. While she went to a public school with her neighbors' kids, she hung with the boy forming a good pair for about two years. When she turned eight years old, she couldn't spend time with him because her family moved to a big house in an upscale neighborhood and Sara put June in a private school. Since then, the memory about him grew dim by losing touch with him. And June made friends in her private school who are mostly arrogant and snobbish.

The cell phone rings and June clicks the On button. As June expects, she hears Sara over the phone.

"Mom, I drove it home nicely. It looks so beautiful. I love it. I texted to dad. Bye for now Mom!" June says and clicks the Hang Up button.

Soon, June climbs into the driver's seat of her Malibu and starts the engine. She drives slowly to the street and keeps driving at a moderate speed. At a certain spot after a half hour driving, she turns the wheel to go back home feeling confident about her driving. While returning home, she speeds up little by little and then makes a sharp turn at a point where the road curves to the right. Though she should have slowed down when turning, she doesn't do it because of her inexperienced driving.

Then she finds a car parked on the shoulder of the road. Despite hitting the brake at once, she can't avoid bumping into the car ahead.

She is panicked and stays in the car thinking what to do. She sees a man come toward her from the car ahead. She rolls down the driver's side window. "I'm sorry. I didn't see your car."

"It's okay. I think there's a little scratch. If you aren't insured, I won't ask anything about the damage. You're free to go," the man says.

"I'm gonna call my insurance agent now. Let me call my

mom first," June says with a grimace.

"Yeah... wait a minute. I see a little scratch, but it doesn't get a dent at all. I'm fine and you're fine. And my car has already got a lot of scratches. I think you can go," the man says.

After feeling safe from the man, June gets out of the car and asks the man's name.

"Don Johnson. Well... excuse me, I should go now."

"Really? But I can't let you go like this. Let me give my number," June says.

"No, it's okay. Bye," Don says, waving his hands.

As Don drives away from the scene, June quickly holds her cell phone and takes a picture of the license plate of Don's car. Then, she checks her car to see if the minor collision left a dent on the right-hand side. She can't find a dent or a scratch. She smiles thinking that her first car may bring good luck to her.

On arriving at the house, June texts Sara, "Mom, I'm home now. You know what? When I drove my car, I had a fender bender. Don't worry. Nothing happened luckily. Keep doing your job and see you at dinner."

She sits on the couch turning on TV, but her eyes falls on her cell phone as usual. While looking over the pictures of the car she bumped into, she understands why Don went away without any claim. The photo shows an old sedan that has a lot of scratches and dents. Feeling a pity on him, she begins to recall the scene of the collision. She thinks that Don about her age looked somewhat familiar, but she shakes her head convincing she hasn't seen him anywhere around her. At that moment June's cell phone vibrates.

"Hi, June, I wonder how you like your car. Can I see it now? If yes, come to my house now," Jennifer says on the cell phone.

"No problem," June says.

She grabs the car key and texts Sara where she's going now. June, the pale-skinned girl with dark brown eyes and dark brown hair, always informs either Sara or John of her whereabouts.

June at the wheel with a bit of confidence this time thinks she'll drive cautiously. As she drives to see Jennifer, she passes a neighborhood where the flats are concentrated along the freeway. When she almost reaches the exit, she finds a broken-down car on the shoulder. She recognizes the car instantly when she passes it by and sees Don Johnson sit in the car. She sighs softly thinking that he has a bad day.

As June enters a rich neighborhood, she sees Jennifer standing on the street in front of her house. Jennifer gets in the passenger seat. "Oh, it looks good. Let's hit the road."

"Alright! Where to?" June asks and turns around heading back the way she came.

"Oh, a car broke down on the other side of the road," Jennifer says, pointing to Don's car.

June doesn't look at it. "What a poor guy! You know, that car was hit by me about an hour ago. But there wasn't any dent at all on both cars."

"Really? What a lucky girl you are, June," Jennifer pats June on the shoulder.

"Well... he must be waiting for a tow car. Jennifer, do you happen to recognize his face?" June asks.

"No. How do I know that kind of guy?" Jennifer says

cutely.

As June and Jennifer enter the mall, they bump into some guys who look gorgeous and rich. One of the guys glances at June, but she ignores him.

"Look, what if I pick one of those guys?" Jennifer asks.

"I think they know you, Jennifer. They go to our school and you're popular," June says, winking at Jennifer.

That evening June and Sara sit at the table for dinner without John Kee who rarely joins them due to a hectic schedule. While having a meal June talks a lot about her car and how she was in a fender bender on her way home including Don.

"Wait a minute. The name sounds familiar. Oh, yes, your buddy..., I think his name was Don. You don't remember the boy's name, do you?" Sara says, tilting her head.

"What? You mean the boy at the public school? Yeah... oh, I get it. That's why he looked familiar. Wow, it's amazing," June shouts.

"June, I didn't say that's him," Sara says.

"Mom, you're right. I think he's Don. Oh, I was a fool. How couldn't I recognize him? And I even didn't get his phone number. I should've asked it," June says with a look of disappointment.

"June, I can be wrong. You know, I just thought of that name off the top of my head, but forget it," Sara says.

While watching June who looks so excited about meeting Don by chance, Sara feels regret that she reminds June of him.

As Sara looks back on June's early childhood days, Sara remembers that June liked so much to do everything with Don no matter what happened feeling sorry for him who had lived with his mother, a single parent. Even though Sara had never been in contact with Don's mother, Sara knew about Don since she volunteered as a room mother in June's class. As far as Sara knew, Don was born to an American father and a Mexican mother who had worked as a waitress. Despite Don's good nature, Sara didn't want June to get along with Don at that time, but she couldn't have any excuse to let June stay away from Don. In the mean time, John Kee earned decent money that he could afford to pay expensive tuition for June. Then Sara decided to move to a wealthier neighborhood and enrolled June at a good private school. Since then Sara hasn't heard about Don and his mother.

June looks at Sara who seems to be in a daze and rises to her feet.

"I'm done, Mom. Are you, too? I'll clean up the table," June says.

"Oh, thanks, sweetie. We can do it together?" Sara rises to her feet too.

Sara and June stand side by side at the kitchen sink. Sara glances at June to see how June looks now, and finds that June will work on a frantic search for Don. Sara sighs quietly thinking that June is getting out of hand.

The sun goes down and darkness falls. Sara sits in the living room without turning on TV and looks tired from her daily workload. While checking her schedule for the next day, Sara sees headlights flickering on the window. Soon, John comes in the front door and says, "I'm hungry to death, Sara."

"Oh, honey, we've just finished dinner. But I'll make a special sandwich for you. Wash your hands," Sara says with a sweet smile.

John starts to eat like a horse and finishes his meal in a blink.

"Oh, you're still here. I bet you have something to say. What is it?" John asks, looking at Sara who still sits next to John.

"John, you read my mind, huh. June loves her car," Sara says.

"I know, honey. She texted me as soon as she got it. And what? Is there anything wrong going on?" John asks with a look of curiosity.

When Sara sees his face, she smiles at him thinking that John is so adorable that she can't stop loving him.

"Not really. I don't think you remember a boy, Don. He had been June's best friend before we moved here. He hasn't kept touch with June since then, but June happened to see him in the afternoon," Sara says.

"So, what's the problem? June can see her friend, can't she?" John says with a look of indifference.

"You're right. It's no big deal. John, how was your day? Busy, huh? We both are so busy that we can't have time together. I wish I were sunbathing on the beach with you," Sara says.

"Yeah, let's make time in the near future," John says, grabbing his cell phone to watch baseball game.

Sara also grabs her phone to keep checking her schedule, saying to herself that she won't bother June regarding Don.

4

Next morning, June opens her eyes as the alarm goes off. She looks around her room as if she is in a strange place. A second ago she was with Don jotting down Don's phone number in a summer house by the lake. All of sudden, there was a sharp toot outside, and she starts from her sleep. June feels so sorry that she couldn't remember Don's phone number.

June sluggishly rises from the bed and goes through her address book just to be sure.

"Come on, June. Use your brain to find Don," June says to herself.

The school parking lot seems to be full, but June finds a place to park. She stands next to her car feeling pride that she finished her first driving to school by parking her car in a narrow space without any scratch. As June walks to the school building, she is blocked by an unfamiliar face and asked. "Excuse me, let me ask you something. Where is the administration office?"

"Are you new here? Follow me. It's in this building," June says.

"I'm not coming this school. I just came to meet a woman. She's working in the office," the girl says.

"Oh, I see. Who is she?" June asks without any meaning.

"Her name is Graciela. I don't think you know her, do you?" the girl asks.

"No, here's the office. Have a nice day," June says and goes to her classroom.

The room is already filled with students, being ready for class. June sits beside Jennifer.

"Hi, Jennifer. You know what? I had a dream about Don. I was about to have his number, but damn alarm made him evaporate," June says.

Jennifer looks at June with awe. "Why are you so interested in him? It's odd. He's nobody to you, June. I don't understand."

"It's not strange. He was my friend I liked so much. But I was stupid 'cause I couldn't recognize him, huh. I wouldn't think of him unless my mom reminded me of my childhood last night," June says.

"Come on, June, don't be ridiculous. Is he your ex? We have plenty of gorgeous boys in here. What are you gonna do this afternoon?" Jennifer asks with her glittering eyes.

Jennifer, who is quite a doll, suggests that they go to see a movie with her boyfriend and his friend. June doesn't have the feel for it, but she nods to Jennifer for now.

After school June heads to a movie theater by her car and reaches the huge parking lot. While roaming to find a space to park, June finds that Jennifer is ahead of her. June pulls over her car next to Jennifer's BMW, and they walk side by side to the entrance. From a few meters away Don is passing them toward another entrance, but June doesn't notice it since she keeps looking at Jennifer's green eyes while chatting and laughing.

In the hall June has had a lively conversation with her

companions until June happens to see Don who is working on a hotdog stand. On seeing Don, her mind goes blank with surprise.

"Look, Jennifer, he's over there. I mean... Don. Oh, what shall I do?" June whispers.

Jennifer looks around the hall and finds a man at a hotdog stand.

"Is he Don? Wow, he's a handsome guy. Now I get it why you would like to see him," Jennifer whispers back.

"Jennifer, do me a favor. Tell your guys that I can't make it to the movie. Tell them I got an urgent call," June whispers.

"Alright, take your time. June, if Don doesn't like to be your boyfriend, pass him to me. I'm kidding. Good luck!" Jennifer whispers back.

June goes to the hotdog stand and stops in front of Don who is ready to take an order.

"May I help you?" Don says looking at June without showing any astonishment.

"Yeah, I want a hotdog with onions only. By the way, are you Don?" June says.

"Yeah? Well... oh, you're... Excuse me, I'm busy right now. Next!" Don ignores June and takes orders from other customers.

"Okay, I'll wait until you're finished..." June says to herself.

It takes almost two hours for Don to have time for June who has been around the hall watching him.

When Don gets out of the stand he sees June sitting on the bench near the hotdog stand. He approaches June. "Excuse me. Why are you waiting for me? Did I do anything wrong yesterday, miss?"

"No, I just wanted to know you're the boy I hung out with. I'm June," June says.

"What? Let me think... well, there was a close friend. You were... my buddy? Oh, I'm so sorry, but you've changed so much. You look so good," Don shouts with surprise.

While watching Don's exaggerated expression, June thinks that he grows up to be a real attractive man.

"Don, I'm so happy to see you again. I've been thinking how I can reach you since last night when I dreamed about you. Oh, my dream came true," June says with a big smile.

"Don, let's exchange numbers. And do you go to high school around here?" June asks.

Don gives his number to June, but doesn't answer her. Instead, he walks toward the parking lot, saying that he has to go on for work. Soon later, June finds that he works all year around to make money for his college. June feels sorry that Don has in poor financial situation.

As June approaches the house that evening, she sees a dim light coming from the living room which is set up to be turned on automatically when nobody is in. After she shuts the garage door, she goes straight to her room. As usual, she sits on the built-in couch by the window, the favorite spot of the room, and looks down at the street where a streetlight throws the garden in shadows. While recalling the heart-stopping moment that she found Don a few hours earlier, she sees Sara's Audi stopped in the driveway. June rises to her feet to go downstairs.

"Hi, Mom. I had a hotdog around 4 o'clock, so I'm not hungry," June says.

"Really? I bought salads and some burgers for you. How was your day?" Sara asks.

"Mom, don't be surprised. I met Don. I couldn't believe my eyes when I saw him at a hotdog stand. He was working at the counter," June says, exciting.

"Wow. It's a surprise. What a small world! So, how's he doing? Where does he live?" Sara shows an interest in Don.

"You know, he was working and I couldn't help waiting. And when his shift was done he had to move to work in another place. So, we just exchanged numbers. That's all. I have to ask him when he's available," June sighs.

Sara feels sorry for June who still has a crush on Don, and reluctantly plans to invite him for dinner to see whether he is qualified to be June's boyfriend.


Several days have passed since June keeps texting every hour to Don though she doesn't have any messages from him. In the meanwhile June gets a phone call.

"Hello, Don? You didn't text me back. What happen to you?"June says, feeling small.

"Hello, this is Alice, Don's cousin. I have to tell you a terrible story. I heard of you from Don a few days ago. Don said he was excited by running into you and he was gonna meet you soon. By the way, things happened. Don is in the hospital because of a car accident. He was struck from the rear by a drunken driver on the way home. He wasn't killed, but he fell into a coma. And this morning I found out that you texted almost every hour. So, I have to tell about Don 'cause I can imagine you'll wait for his answer every minute. I'm so sorry," Alice says with heavy voice.

June becomes speechless for a while. She seems to be so shocked that she can't come up with a word.

"Hmm... that's why I can't have his answer. Just before you called me I thought he didn't wanna speak with me. What a horrible thing happened to him!" June says, sobbing.

"June, you can come over the hospital. My aunt is in grief so much, but she doesn't think his life ends like this," Alice says.

"Which hospital is he in? I'm gonna see him right now. Is there a specific visiting hour?" June asks, grabbing her car key.

The sky is filled with thick rain clouds as if it is about to pour torrential rain. June gets in her car and texts to Sara who went to play golf in the indoor lounge with John. June doesn't write about Don, but mentions where she's going. Without paying attention to the weather June starts the car and takes the freeway to get to the hospital. She drives as fast as she can in the heavy rain, thinking of Don only. She doesn't seem to know that she should have to be careful in driving on the freeway as a novice driver.

June hurries to the information desk to ask which room Don is staying in. In the elevator she takes a deep breath to be ready to face Don who has been in a coma, holding her pounding heart. While walking down the hall to find Don who is supposed to be on life support, she's being tapped on the shoulder and turns around.

"Oh, Don, you're awake. What a big surprise! Are you okay? Gosh, you're normal. What happen to you? I've been so terrified on my way, but you walk. Anyway, I'm talking with you at last. I'm so glad to see you," June says joyfully.

"Yep, I'm glad to see you too, June. I've been thinking of you. And I'm sorry I couldn't text you. Will you forgive me? Yeah... you were always on my side and did everything for me. I remember all about us now," Don says with a big smile.

His attractive smile drives June crazy enough to hold him tight. But June just smiles back at Don.

"Hey, if you can walk, let's go out. We don't have to stay here. Come and hold my hand," June says.

Holding hands, they move through the wall instead of passing the big glass door. Since June feels so excited with Don, she doesn't notice that Sara and John are seated on a bench in front of the hospital building and walks past them. June seems to be delighted to be led to somewhere by Don. A while later June finds that they are in Don's place where he shares with his roommate, Brent.

"Oh, you don't live with your mom. Anyway I was wondering how you're living. Here it is... an old picture of you. You were so cute," June says.

"Really? Thanks. June, what do you wanna do? I can go everywhere with you 'cause I'm free," Don says.

June looks Don into his eyes without blinking her eyes and nods her head. "How about going to the beach?"

"Alright," Don says.

"It takes a couple of hours, I guess. Don, you'd better drive my car," June says, trying to think where she parked it.

"By the way, I can't remember how we got to your place. Can you tell me?" June asks.

Don shakes his head.

"June, forget it. Let's walk as we did from the hospital. We can reach as fast as we can if we think of the beach," Don says with smile.

"What do you mean? You mean we can fly or what? But I believe you, Don."

June feels strange while looking at her feet which are floating a little above the ground. But she doesn't care about it as long as she is with Don. And she thinks that she'll enjoy the moments that may go away in any minutes.

As they are heading to the beach, they are surrounded pretty birds that sing songs and a kind of music June hasn't heard before. June feels light and easy with Don, and forgets Sara and John who will be freaked out if they know June disappears with Don. June shrugs her shoulder and says to herself, "I'm a grown up. I can go everywhere I want to."

Sara and John leave the room where June is on a life support machine. They both are frustrated with themselves since they can't do anything for June. Remaining tight lipped, they walk to the hospital door past Maria who stands against them at the information desk. When Maria turns around from the counter and sees them, they have just walked outside the door.

They approach the parking lot, and John opens his mouth looking at Sara's swollen eyes. "Sara, it's really hard to see June in a coma. But I believe June's gonna be okay. She'll get up and hug us soon. I know we're so helpless right now. Luckily, she wasn't injured in the accident. So, when she gets up, she'll be our June again. Oh, God..."

Sara gets in her car to go to work and says without looking

at John. "See you at home, John. I love you."

While driving to work, Sara feels uncomfortable and even angry. She shakes her head as if she can't accept the terrible thing that happened to June, trying to get rid of the words "in serious condition" ringing in her head which she heard from the policeman who was at the scene of the car accident. As she knew that June was on her way to Don in such a bad weather after getting a phone call, she became upset with June. She could imagine that June was driving too fast to control her wheel which slid to the shoulder lane and had hit her head on the handle before the airbag popped up. In consequence, June fainted and fell into a coma. The whole thing that happened to June was unbearable to Sara. Besides, Sara found that June's next door neighbor in the hospital was Don when she ran into Graciela, Don's mother, who was walking out of Don's room. That was another shock to Sara as an odd coincidence. The more Sara thinks about June, the more complicated she feels. On one hand, Sara feels like punishing Alice who Sara thinks must be the cause of June's car crash.

Sara gets to the office and sits at her computer for her daily routine. Soon, she focuses on her job getting away from the things about June. Once in a while she checks her cell phone to see there are new messages. She sighs whenever she takes a break, and Maria comes to Sara with a look of anxiety.

"Sara, relax! I'm so sorry that June fell into a coma. I know how you feel. I feel the same. You know, she's like my granddaughter. But, it's no use to regret or feel sad. God will do for June, and she will be fine. I believe it," Maria says.

"Oh, Maria. I hope so. I know there's nothing we can do, but I feel so angry about Alice and Don. Did you text to Lan about June?" Sara says.

"No, she shouldn't know this. She would be freaked out and get sick if she heard about June. We'd better be quiet to Lan," Maria says, looking at Sara in the eyes.

Oddly enough, Sara sees something from Maria for the first time ever, and then thinks Maria may know something about Don because Maria looks like Graciela in some way.

"Sara, Don is a poor kid," Maria says without blinking her eyes.

"What? Oh, do you know him? Why didn't you say you

knew Don?" Sara asks with a curious look.

"Sara, I didn't know June was his friend 'cause I've never heard about Don until now. Obviously, I found June and Don went to school together for a couple of years when I visited June in the hospital. Sara, Graciela is my daughter, but I live by myself. Since you hired me, I didn't have to tell my family matters as you know," Maria takes a deep breath.

"Oh, what a surprise! I've never thought you were related. Anyway I didn't get along with Graciela, so I wasn't interested in her life. But I know you, and as long as Don is your grandson, he must be a good boy," Sara says, smiling a bit.

"It's a small world anyway. But why do these horrible things happen to June and Don? I don't understand. I really don't..." Sara embraces her face feeling so complicated.

One evening, after almost two weeks have passed since June fell into a coma, John comes home earlier than Sara. He goes upstairs to June's room and sits on a built-in couch. He looks around the room in which everything is in place. He says to himself. "She's my girl. She can't mess up around. She learned from me though I didn't teach her. Oh, please, June, wake up. Then I'll spend more time with you."

John goes out of the room when he hears someone coming upstairs. To his surprise, June stands with bare feet in front of him. He shouts with extreme shock. "Oh, June, you're home. What a miracle!"

"Dad, did you see Don here? We were heading to the beach, but he disappeared suddenly. I can't find him right now.

Oh my gosh! Where did he go? Dad, I'll talk to you later," June leaves in a hurry.

John stands still for a minute and hears Sara getting in the kitchen.

"I'm home, John. Are you upstairs?"

"I'm coming. Honey, did you see June close the door to the kitchen?" John asks.

"What? Are you crazy? She's not here. I even didn't hear anything. Oh, John, you're hallucinating, I guess. Come on!" Sara says with wide-eyed.

Soon, Sara takes off her jacket and begins to prepare supper. She feels free from anxiety for a while. Sara and John finish dinner in a quiet mood. They try to avoid talking about June, but John brings up the presence of June.

"Sara, it was real. I mean June came to me and talked. She said she was looking for Don who was gone while they were heading to the beach," John says.

"Honey, okay, I believe you. But you'd better call the hospital and ask how June's doing."

"John, I tell you what. Don is Maria's grandson. Can you

believe it? I couldn't believe my ears. I think many things are happening after June got her car. The car brings June's old friend and unexpected truth. I've never imagined Maria is Don's grandmother, huh."

"Come to think of it, you're saying repeatedly about Don. Who is Don?" John asks.

"Don is June's childhood friend. Since June happened to see him on the day when she got her car, she seems to have chased him. John, our daughter has a crush on him. Oh, hell! She had no chance to spend time with him. They are just lying side by side," Sara sighs heavily.

"Yeah, that makes sense. That's why June was looking for Don. What if something's going on in the unconscious world? She might come to me to show something. Anyway, I wish June could awake from her coma," John say.

"You're saying her spirit appeared to you to say something. Oh, boy! It's no use arguing with you. Let it go for now. We'd better go to see her at the hospital the first thing in the morning," Sara says, yawning.

Sara and John go to bed early at night feeling exhausted. Sara pulls the sheet over her face when John grabs a book from the side table. In a minute Sara falls asleep and John tries to feel sleepy by reading a history book. After turning a few pages, John becomes wide awake thinking of June. At that moment John sees June coming through the wall. He can't believe his eyes.

"Hey, June, are you ghost? How can you move through the wall? You're supposed to be in the hospital," John says.

"Dad, I'm okay now. You know, I was looking for Don. I found him in his place, but he became dumb. And he even ignored me as if I was invisible. I think I have to let him go," June says with sad eyes.

It is heartbreaking to see June losing heart.

"Oh, June, don't be silly. Wait. Let's go to his place. I'll talk to him," John says.

John gets in his car waiting for June, but she doesn't show up. He looks out the car window and turns back to see June is behind. He finds that there is no one around. He mumbles, "Am I hallucinating again? Sara must be right."

Sara's cell phone alarm goes off at the dawn of the next day. She springs up from the bed and wakes John who is in deep sleep. Sara seems to be in a good mood. When Sara and John sit at the kitchen table for breakfast, Sara makes a big smile for the first time since June fell into a coma.

"John, I had a good dream last night, and I feel like that June starts to awake from a coma. I think she'll get well," Sara says.

"I wish your dream will come true. Are you finished? Then let's go," John says.

Sara arrives at the hospital before John and pushes an elevator button without waiting for John. As Sara enters it, a woman behind says, "Excuse me."

Sara turns around and sees Graciela.

"Oh, you're early too. How's Don? I hope our June and Don will recover as soon as possible," Sara says.

"I believe they'll recover some day. We just have to wait with a prayer. How are you doing? It's been almost eight years after you moved," Graciela says.

"Yeah. Though we were not friends, June was close to Don. Is it a coincidence or what? It's really odd. I really don't know how June encountered Don in a fender bender about two weeks ago when she drove her first car," Sara says.

"I had no idea what was going on. Don has lived with his friend, and we don't talk much because Don's so busy. Though I haven't pushed him to work that hard, he doesn't listen to me and his father. Since his father remarried, Don has avoided him. His father doesn't know Don is in a coma," Graciela says.

"Oh, I happen to know you began to work in Sara's school lately. It may be good for you. The job in school office is stable," Sara says.

As they keep talking in the hallway, Sara sees John stand in the room. Sara gets in the room and looks into June to see if June has changed a bit by recalling her dream in which June woke up and held Sara. Without saying anything Sara holds June's hand and pats it. Suddenly, Sara feels a mere trembling on her fingers.

"Oh my gosh! John, June moves her finger. Here! Touch her now. Do you feel it?" Sara shouts.

"Oh, my! She's moving her finger. Nurse! Nurse! She's coming back," John shouts too.

A nurse calls the doctor to let him check June's condition. The doctor checks if June can breathe without life support, and finds that she does it by herself. He orders the nurse to remove June's respirator and says that he will watch June who is still lying with her eyes closed. Sara and John hug each other tightly weeping tears of joy.

"Oh, Sara, your dream came true. By the way, you know, I hallucinated last night. I mean June came to me, but disappeared soon. I guess her spirit went back to her body," John says.

After making sure that June is getting well, Sara goes to the next room where Graciela sits beside Don who still is kept on life support.

"Graciela, I bet Don will wake up soon," Sara says, patting Graciela's shoulder.

"Yes, I believe so. And I'm so happy for you, Sara. Thank you for caring about Don," Graciela says.

June is released from the hospital after having a checkup with her physician. On the ride home June stays quiet in the passenger seat next to Maria. After getting off the car, June smiles at Maria. "Thanks a lot, Maria. Hmm… I'm home at last."

"Congrats June! I'm so happy for you. See you around. Bye now," Maria says with a smile and turns her car around.

"June doesn't seem to know I'm Don's grandma," she mumbles.

As soon as June gets inside the house, she goes straight to her room and sits on the built-in couch by the window. Looking down at her Malibu which is in the driveway being repaired, she recalls the stormy day. If the phone call wasn't about Don, she wouldn't drive out to the freeway. She smiles to herself picturing how dauntless she was that afternoon in running to him. But in a minute she feels blue as she thinks of Don.

Before June bumped into Don, she had never dreamed of meeting him. However, after Sara reminded June of Don, the events of her childhood days as well as her feeling for him rose at once in her memory, and June began to fall into him uncontrollably. Now June heartily wants to get close to Don. She thinks that Don is the ordinary good looking guy she has looked for since the teenage boys in her school are too rich to be serious.

As John and Sara come back home from work, all three family members sit around the table for June's first welcome-home dinner. Sara and John raise their hands and begin to clap hard.

"June. Welcome back home. We're so happy to have you back," John says. "June, by the way, do you remember you appeared in the house twice?"

"No, I don't. What I dreamed was that I was walking with Don holding his hand. But it happened for a few seconds. Why is that?" June says without looking her parents.

"Forget it. But I'm sure I saw you while you were in a coma. Your mom said I hallucinated. Anyway it doesn't matter. You're here with us," John says, smiling at June.

"Dad, Mom. How come Don doesn't wake up? Is there any ways to help him? I feel bad for him," June say with anxiety.

"June, guess what! Maria is Don's grandma. Isn't it surprise?" Sara says.

"What? I can't believe it. I wonder why she didn't say it on the way home," June says with wide eyes.

As they finish dinner, June gets a message from Jennifer.

"Mom, can I go to see Don tomorrow after school? Jennifer wants to see him," June asks Sara.

"Yes, honey, if you aren't be tired. It'll be a bit hard to stay in school all day after a long break. So, promise me this. Don't step on it when driving," Sara says.

*10*

June arrives at school earlier than usual. She looks around the school feeling complicated emotions when she thinks about her experience of falling into a coma. She drops by the school office to see Graciela as she heard about Don's mother from Sara. She stands in front of Graciela. "Hello, here I am. How are you doing?"

"Oh, you're back to school. It's good to see you healthy. I'm happy for you," Graciela smiles at June.

While talking with her, she finds out that Don looks exactly like his mother. She is a gorgeous woman with tenderness. Thinking of Sara who might be jealous of her beauty, June smiles to herself. June remembers that Sara looked down on Graciela due to her educational background along with her divorce. Now June thinks the reason that Sara has been reluctant to admit Don as June's friend must be Graciela's looking.

"Mrs. Johnson, I'm gonna see Don at the hospital. I wanna do anything I can do for him," June says.

"Call me Graciela. Thanks a lot, June. You're so sweet," Graciela says, smiling.

Thinking that Graciela looks younger than her age, June walks to the classroom.


After school, June gets off the school parking lot toward the street. When she is about to turn around to enter the freeway, she pushes the brake quickly and pulls the car onto the shoulder to see the man who is walking along the road with his thumb up because he seems to be Don. She watches him with doubt in her eyes.

"Oh my gosh! Is he Don? It can't happen. He's in his sickbed. Oh... Am I hallucinating as my dad did? Anyway, I'll take him in the car," June says to herself.

June stops next to Don and sees him move in through the

passenger door. She feels her heart flip.

"Hi, Don. Oh, I didn't expect to see you here. What a surprise!" June tries to calm down.

"Hi, June, you look good. I have something to tell you. I was going to my place 'cause I have something to do," Don says.

"What is it? I'll do it for you. But I don't know where you're living," June says, catching sight of a patrol car in the rear view mirror.

The patrol car stops behind June's car.

"Hello, miss, what are you doing here alone? Any trouble with your car? If not, you can't park here. Please move your car," the patrol officer says.

"Alright, I'm moving. Thank you," June says, glancing at the passenger seat.

June sees no one sit on the passenger seat, and she drives to the hospital to meet Jennifer.

June and Jennifer stand at Don's sickbed looking down at him. He looks normal unless being kept on life support.

"Jennifer, I didn't know you'd liked to see Don. But I appreciate your attention to him. Oh, poor Don! I really want him to be back to his old self," June says blinking her eyes.

"Yeah. By the way, do you think I have a crush on him? No, I don't. But I'm definitly interested in him because he's one of your friends. You know, we share everything together," Jennifer says, staring at Don.

"Speaking of sharing, I've got something to tell you. You know what? Don was with me in my car for a moment. He was hitchhiking near the freeway and got in my car. It sounds odd, but I think his ghost came to me. It's meant to be his communication," June says.

"Really? His body's here, but his spirit travels, huh. Then his ghost appears where he's used to, I guess. June, do you know where he lives?" Jennifer asks.

"How do I know it? I just have his cell phone number. That's it. And I texted him tons of times without knowing he was in a car crash," June says, sighing.

"You know his mother, and we can ask her about her address," Jennifer says, blinking her eyes.

"No, he lives alone with his roommate. And Graciela didn't know exactly where he lived. I know it doesn't make sense, but it's true," June says.

Luckily, Jennifer's father has a connection with a phone company that is likely to figure out Don's address. A couple of days later, June can make it to Don's place with Jennifer.

June and Jennifer arrives at the neighborhood which was crowded with flat-roofed, narrow, two-story houses, a separate apartment on each floor. They try to seek in which apartment Don lives while parking in the street with the engine idling. Since they don't want to bump into people in the neighborhood, they have hesitated to get out of the car. At that moment they see a cat coming, and it seems to feel at ease. As they still stay inside the car, a man walks to the cat calling its name and it begins to rub the man's hand with its forefeet. The man gives the cat bits of food and goes on his way.

"June, he looks like a nice guy. But he's a stranger. Okay, let's move on to find Don's place. Wait a minute, we're right here to see if Don's ghost appears to us. But if it doesn't happen, and instead if we're attacked and robbed... oh, I'm afraid," Jennifer says.

Listening to Jennifer about being robbed and attacked, June comes up with a wild idea. She recalls what John, her dad, said at the dinner table. According to John, her spirit appeared to John, while her body lay in a coma in the hospital. June's ghost showed up with a look of anxiety to ask where she could find Don at first and disappeared with a look of desperation after being hurt by the coldness in Don's attitude. From all accounts June heard, she concludes that her spirit appeared in the form of a ghost to get help and returned to her body to breathe on her own when feeling suffocated due to tremendous despair. Then she imagines that Don's ghost may show up when June gets in trouble in his place, and Don may wake up out of a coma when his spirit can feel completely helpless.

June turns her face and looks at Jennifer. "Hey, you may be right. We can be in trouble if we get out of my car. We'd better go home now. Besides, we're not sure Don's ghost will appear here. Now that we know this neighborhood, we can come back with guys."

That night June can't sleep as she thinks more and more about her plan which seems to be simple. She just goes to Don's place alone to call Don's ghost that may show up if she is at stake. This plan is obviously her own personal solution, not related with a medical solution, and June is sure that this plan is the only way she can try to get Don back to normal although she will put herself in danger and her effort may not lead to a good result. However, June really wants to help Don by all means to make him break out of his coma as soon as possible.

June makes up her mind to go to Don's house alone sooner or later without texting to Jennifer or to her parents. Considering Jennifer's involvement in June's plan, June doesn't intend to count Jennifer in Don's matter due to her chicken-heartedness. Since Jennifer has never been through any difficulties in her wealthy life, June knows that Jennifer's timid disposition sometimes turns out to be nastier in an unexpected situation.

As June spends a few days delaying her plan to put into action, June has a dream that she meets Don in his place with his roommate, Brent. Don looks sad while Brent is talking a lot with a strange smile. June can't stand listening to Brent, so she tries to stop him. Suddenly Brent comes at her and puts a gag in her mouth and tries to take her to the bed. She begins to struggle and then she wakes up.

Next morning, June thinks that it's time to carry out her plan since Don in his sickbed doesn't get better at all. June tries to feel confident in her plan although she is going to face a personal crisis on her own initiative without any help from her parents and Maria.

June has been nervous all day in school. On hearing the bell which rings at the end of class, June takes her stuff and walks down the hallway. When she sees Jennifer in the distance, she just gestures to Jennifer that she hurries to her car.

About thirty minutes later June turns the engine off in the parking lot and heads to Don's apartment. After taking a deep breath to calm down, June knocks on the door. There doesn't seem to be nobody inside. June goes back to her car to wait for Don's roommate whom she saw last night in her dream. In the car, the silence seems to increase a sense of uneasiness. June tries to cheer herself up and keep thinking about Don to put a positive spin on her visit to his place. As it stands now, her situation shows that Don's recovery becomes her ultimate goal in life.

The clock is ticking, but June can't see any passerby in the parking lot. Then a man comes toward her car and knocks on the car window.

June rolls down the window a little and looks up at him.

"Hello, you've been here once, right? I saw you and another girl in this car. Are you looking for someone?" the man asks.

"Yes, I'm wondering if you know Don. I know his house number, but..." June says with a low voice.

"Oh, yeah..." the man says and walks away from the car toward the one of the two story houses.

Only then does June recognize the man, the one that came near her car to feed a stray cat several days ago. He looks like a regular guy in his early 20s, and June doesn't feel threatened by him. After he disappears from sight, June stays in the car for a little while. Finally June steps out of the car without her cell phone because she knows what Sara and Maria will do if June doesn't text back to them in ten minutes. She takes the stair to reach Don's place. As soon as June knocks on the door, it opens. To her surprise the man she talked to is in front of June.

"Oh, you're the..." June mumbles.

"Yes, here I am. I'm Brent, Don's roommate. I didn't expect you here. By the way what brings you here? Don isn't home. Do you know what happened to Don?" the man says without inviting June inside.

June flinches when she is told that his name is the same one as in her dream.

"No, but can I come in for a minute?" June says casually.

June gets inside the house and Brent, the man, looks at June with a look of suspicion. He seems to think that June is a undercover detective although she looks young.

"Well, can you tell me what's happening to Don? Where is he? He's supposed to be home," June says.

"Don hasn't been around for a month. I need him to pay a rent, but he doesn't answer me. Are you his friend? He hasn't mentioned about you at all," Brent says, standing against an old worn couch.

"So, what do you want from Don?" Brent asks staring at June.

June doesn't answer him, instead she walks to the kitchen and sits at the kitchen table. June looks around the small kitchen finding a coffee maker on.

"May I have a cup of coffee, please? I have something to ask about Don," June asks the man for a cup of coffee.

She feels scared enough to want to run out of the house, but she presses her lips together to fight fear and puts on a brave face for Brent.

Brent sits at the kitchen table across June after serving coffee. June sips coffee glancing at him. About ten minutes after June has a little conversation with Brent, June begins to feel strange leaving her memory hazy. She tries to rise to her feet to move forward, but she falls to her knees, and then she collapses on the floor. While lying down on the floor, June sees what Brent is doing to her since she doesn't fall asleep. He puts her on the chair and ties her wrists behind the backrest. Then he quickly takes out her personal stuff from her purse and spills everything on the floor. He grabs her car key with all the cash June has, and he shuts the door behind her. June feels dumbfounded because it happens in the blink of an eye.

June shouts to get help, but her tongue feels numb and

can't stand up with her wrists tied on the back of the chair. At last June realizes how stupid she is. She was so dauntless in trying to save Don in the fantasy that there is a ghost thing she can call on her own way. She should have consulted with her parents and Maria before she put her ridiculous plan into action, especially with John because he had experienced something such as June's ghost. As June is at a loss what to do, she sits helpless feeling drowsy and begins to doze off.

An hour or so has passed before June comes to herself. June opens her eyes to look around and sees Don stand in front of her. She throws back her head with a startle, but soon figures out where she is and gives him a big smile.

Don just looks down at her and says, "June, what are you doing here? Brent did this to you?"

"Yeah, right. He took my car and cash. Are you asking why I'm here? Huh, you told me you wanted to go to your place. So, I thought if I'm here, you're coming to see me. I know it sounds ridiculous, and it's a dumb idea," June grins.

June sees Don look sad while listening to June.

"Don, will you untie my hands? I can't do it by myself," June says.

Don tries to grab the string, but his hands go through it. He finds that his hands can't even hold any objects because every part of his body scatters when it touches things.

"June, Brent isn't that bad though he took some money. I have no idea why he did that to you. He works night shift at a factory. He might have some place to go with your car," Don says.

"Really? Then he could ask me to borrow my car and shouldn't have to tie me like this. I think he's going to get rid of me. Oh, I was a fool," June cries.

A few minutes pass while June calms herself down. As June knows that Don's ghost can't do anything to free her, she wants to talk with him spending some quality time together. She looks up at Don who is still standing. "Now that we're here together, tell me about how you have been. I really wanna know about you, Don. I heard about you getting involved in so many works to make money. Graciela said you began to estrange yourself from your dad since he remarried. Oh, you know she's working in the administration office of my school."

Don tells June about how he had been since June moved to another school. He speaks slowly so that June can notice he doesn't sound normal. While listening to Don, June recalls her childhood when she treated Don like her brother by taking care of everything for him. For these days June doesn't know if her current feeling for him will develop into love. The one thing she focuses on is to help Don get his life back.

At the same time in June's house, Sara goes upstairs to check if June is sleeping since there was no message from June and she even didn't take Sara's calls. Sara begins to feel nervous blaming herself about neglecting June's usual text messages about her whereabouts although she was too busy all day at work. It has never happened so that Sara can't calm down herself.

"Hi, Jennifer, this is Sara. Are you with June now?"

"No, I'm not. June left school in a hurry. So I thought I would talk to her later," Jennifer says.

"Oh my gosh! Where is she? She hasn't texted me where to go after school. This is the first time. I was too busy to notice this. Did you get any message from her?" Sara says, panicked.

"Let me see... oh, my gosh! She might go to the

neighborhood we have been to," Jennifer says.

"What do you mean by that? What neighborhood? Text me where it is and the specific address she might go, please. What on earth is she doing? Her cell phone went off so that I can't reach her," Sara shouts.

At that moment John and Maria get in the house, asking what is going on. Sara explains that June must have disappeared whatever happened. John and Maria look panicked, and John tells Sara about a phone tracking app.

"John, I already tracked her phone, but I can't track the location. It makes me feel frustrated," Sara is about to burst into tears.

Then, Sara's cell phone rings.

"Okay, I get it. I'll be right there with John. Thanks a lot, Jennifer," Sara hangs up the cell phone.

It is almost dusk when John drives to Don's place with Sara after being informed by Jennifer.


Meanwhile, trapped in Don's house, June has come upon a critical moment when Brent returns with a mean face and tries to take her somewhere. This time he puts a gag on June before he carries her. On the other hand, Don becomes frantic to stop Brent, but his incorporeal body can't do anything to protect June. Besides, Don is visible only to June. Don screams at the top of his lungs and uses up all his power to hold Brent.

At that moment John and Sara stand at the door which is slightly open. They push the door lightly to see inside and find June bound and gagged on the chair. At once, they run into the kitchen to save June without observing Brent who runs away. While they are busy freeing June from her captivity as fast as possible, June watches Don fade away in a second with a hope of Don's rising from his sickbed.

Right after John called the police to report about both the car theft and the attempted kidnap of June, Maria and Jennifer arrive at the house and meet June who sits on the chair exhausted. They drop their jaws with a surprise. They look so shocked that their feet seem to be stuck on the floor for a few minutes. Maria walks forward to hold June.

"Oh, June, John and Sara got you back. That was a close

call. Excuse me..." Maria stops talking and turns around to take her cell phone.

While June hears Maria shout with joy, she wonders if Don will be able to breathe on her own. For a second June doubts that her idea really come true because it was too unrealistic to be for real. By the way June hears Maria declare that Don awakened from the coma a few minutes ago and his breathing tube was going to be removed.

"What a miracle! I believed so. Oh, thank you God for giving Don back to us," Maria exclaims.

June doesn't seem to believe the news although she made a plan and put herself in danger.

"What? Amazing! Oh, I'm so happy for you, Maria. I wanna see Don right now. Dad, Mom, let's get out of here," June says with a look of satisfaction.

15

June by sitting in the back seat of John's Mercedes sees the sun go down while looking out the car window. She feels pride at her success that she planned on her own and could achieve with guts as she recalls every moment of what she has gone through. She remembers how she was desperate to do something in her own way for Don no matter what it costs her, which is totally groundless. Occasionally, June hears John speak about how much they were worried about June, being asked why she had to come to Don's place, and she knows they don't expect any answer from her.

After pulling the car in the driveway of their house, John informs June that the police are on the trail of the man who drove off in June's Malibu. Then he turns around to look at

June and says, smiling.

"June, I think you'd better take a rest right now. You have a plenty of time to meet Don. Let's have pizza for dinner. I placed an order and Maria and Jennifer will join us."

"Alright, Dad. It sounds good to me. Yeah, I need a rest after pizza," June says.

John and Sara feel relaxed after getting their only daughter back home safe without a scratch. While having pizza together with Maria and Jennifer, Sara lifts her glass of beer to celebrate the rescue of June and Don's recovery.

"To June! To Don!" Sara makes a toast.

"This is the happiest time in my life. June, I'm so glad to see you safe. By the way, I really wonder the coincidence of June's rescue and Don's recovery. Oh, God saved June and Don," Maria exclaims, rejoicing.

Next morning June wakes up out of a dead sleep. After all three family members in the house have breakfast, Sara takes June to school in her Audi.

During the day at school June feels the fresh air around

her. As soon as her last class has let out in the afternoon, June walks fast to Maria who has been waiting for her. When Maria is about to leave to the hospital with June, Jennifer waves her hand to get the car to stop. June rolls down the car window.

"Hey, June, can I come? I'll drive you back home," Jennifer says, gesturing to Maria with a friendly salute.

"Yeah, I'll see you at the hospital," June says.

June can feel her heart pounding while walking down the hallway to see Don. It takes almost a month for her to meet him in real life since they exchanged their numbers. June can't imagine how Don will react to June. She enters Don's room and finds him laughing aloud whenever Jennifer makes a joke.

"Jennifer, you're already here. You drove fast, huh," June sourly says.

"Yep, couldn't wait. So..." Jennifer glances at June.

"Hey, Don, how are you? You look completely normal. When are you gonna get out of this room?" June says, a bit begrudgingly.

Don seems to know nothing about what June has gone through in his place. Suddenly, June wants to hide from him who looked close to Jennifer and didn't welcome June. June feels disappointed too much and begins to feel sorry for her efforts.

Don starts the rest of his high school life with Graciela in her house after getting out of the hospital. Graciela looks like the happiest mother in the world because she got her son back and put her life on track. Maria, still working for Sara, looks better than ever. John and Sara work hard enjoying their expanding assets. However, June feels blue everyday in warm autumn sunshine.

As Don doesn't remember anything about what happened during the coma, June has some hard feelings toward Don. She doesn't feel regret about awakening Don from the coma by putting herself at risk. She doesn't even more want to be prized for what she went through to save Don. The only thing she wants is for Don to be able to remember about the events which bonded Don's spirit and June.

Being tired of feeling frustrated because Don treats June as his childhood friend, June decides to wipe Don from her mind. While focusing on her study and enjoying driving her new Volvo which is a gift from Sara, June begins to feel comfortable seeing Don with Jennifer who keeps approaching Don to make him like her.


One crisp autumn day June sees a compact car park in front of her house. To her surprise, Don gets out of the car. June runs downstairs to open the front door.

"Hi, Don. What's up?" June asks.

"Hi, I wanna talk to you for a minute. Do you have time?"

"Sure, come in! I'll get you some drink," June says.

"I'm good, thanks. Have a seat. I heard about your visit to my former place. My grandma said you were being held captive and my roommate took your car. Why were you there?" Don asks with a look of curiosity.

June looks at Don for a moment and shows bruises on her wrist.

"Don, look at this. But you don't remember you were with me to help, do you? I know you were in a coma, kept on life support. I mean your spirit came to rescue me. You can't believe it. You think I hallucinated, don't you?" June says.

Don looks June in the eyes for a few minutes. Suddenly, he shakes his head with his eyes wide open with amazement.

"June! You were... oh, they weren't dreams. I thought I had dreams. I walked around with you. One day I went to my place and saw you. You were tied to the backrest, so I tried to free you from Brent. But it was no use. Then, all of a sudden I could breathe some air into my lung by myself. Oh my God!" Don says with a big surprise.

"Yeah, now you remember. I have no idea how I dared to try to have your spirit show up as a ghost in the form of you. Nobody will believe me," June smiles at Don.

"Yeah, they'll say that you make up a story. Anyway, thank you so much, June. I owe you my life," Don says, smiling an attractive smile with his eyes.

Don rises to his feet and goes to the door.

"June, let's talk later. I have to work, you know."

"Sure," June says.

Don hugs June tightly and whispers, "I like you and thanks again."